COWCH

Remole Control

Media Storage Rackoon

BeaVo and RayStation

MAGPIE

WELCOME BAT

Jeremy's house is full of extra animals. Can you find them all?

Kangaroom

MICROWAVE

CHIMPNEY

BEARBECUE

BACK · PERCH

BIG·
BED
WOLF

HAMPSTER

GABULL

HARECASE

BOARWAY

SATELLITE FISH

LIGHTBULBBLE FISH

Quailt

SNAILBOX

WHALEPAPER

ANIMAL HOUSE

Candace Ryan

illustrations by Nathan Hale

Walker & Company

New York

Refrigergator

First published in the United States of America in August 2010 by
Walker Publishing Company, Inc., a division of Bloomsbury Publishing, Inc.
Visit Walker & Company's Web site at www.bloomsburykids.com

For information about permission to reproduce selections from this book, write to
Permissions, Walker & Company, 175 Fifth Avenue, New York, New York 10010

Library of Congress Cataloging-in-Publication Data
Ryan, Candace.
Animal house / by Candace Ryan ; illustrated by Nathan Hale.
p.   cm.
Summary: Jeremy's teacher tells him he belongs in a zoo, but when she pays a home visit
she learns how close that is to the truth as she sees the floormingos, a refrigergator,
armapillows, and other living things that make up his house.
ISBN 978-0-8027-9828-2 (hardcover) • ISBN 978-0-8027-9829-9 (reinforced)
[1. Dwellings—Fiction. 2. Imaginary creatures—Fiction. 3. Teachers—Fiction. 4. Humorous stories.] I. Hale, Nathan, ill. II. Title.
PZ7.R9477Ani 2010   [E]—dc22   2009028787

Book design by Danielle Delaney
Typeset in Myriad Std Tilt
Art created with Golden Acrylic on Crescent board

Printed in China by Hung Hing, Shenzhen, Guangdong
2 4 6 8 10 9 7 5 3 1 (hardcover)
2 4 6 8 10 9 7 5 3 1 (reinforced)

All papers used by Walker & Company are natural, recyclable products
made from wood grown in well-managed forests. The manufacturing processes
conform to the environmental regulations of the country of origin.

Candace Ryan would like to extend special thanks to
Stacy Cantor, Nathan Hale, and Kelly Sonnack.

To Clarke, my favorite imaginician
—C. R.

To my nephews, Elias and Elias
—N. H.

Toucan of Soda

My teacher says I belong in a zoo, and she isn't far from the truth. I live in an animal house. Well, actually, it's a gorvilla.

But Mrs. Nuddles doesn't like any of my stories.

There was the one about my snailbox eating the class plant, and the one about my shrewler gnawing on my Statue of Liberty project.

But I think the one about my vulchair eating my homework pushed her over the edge.

"Jeremy, your overactive imagination has just earned you a home visit. If I don't like what I find, then you won't be going on the field trip with us."

I told Mrs. Nuddles that she couldn't miss my house. It has the biggest condoor in the whole neighborhood. I asked him to be on his best behavior—I really want to go on that field trip tomorrow.

I think I see Mrs. Nuddles through the windodo now.

"Hi, Mrs. Nuddles. Be careful stepping onto the floormingos. They don't like dirt getting stuck between their feathers."

"Oh my," she says with a gasp.

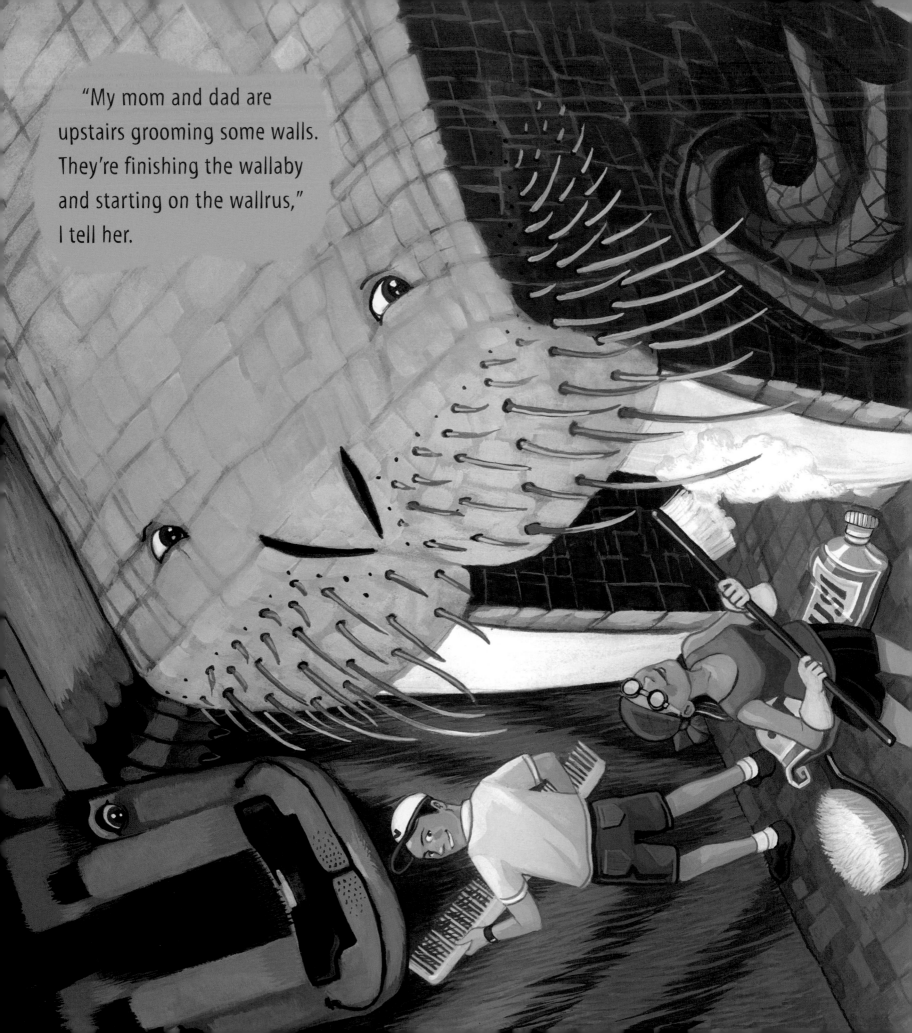

"My mom and dad are upstairs grooming some walls. They're finishing the wallaby and starting on the wallrus," I tell her.

"Grooming some walls?"
Mrs. Nuddles asks.
"Yeah, otherwise Jamie's
toys get stuck in all the snarls."

"Whoa, look out!" I yell.

Jamie left the skink running, and it knocks Mrs. Nuddles up toward the sealing. The chandeldeer tries to catch her, but his antlers get stuck in the sealing's whiskers.

Luckily, one of our armapillows comes to her rescue.

"Why, thank you," Mrs. Nuddles says, straightening her dress.

"That's strike one, Jeremy,"
she says. My hands get sweaty.

"So where is this vulchair that supposedly
ate your homework?"

"In my kangaroom," I tell her. What I don't
tell her is that my vulchair loves to eat really old
things, like Mrs. Nuddles.

I don't want Mrs. Nuddles to see my dad's elepants and my mom's zebras roaming around. I'm supposed to put my dirty clothes in the hampster, but my parents don't always follow that rule.

"Good grief!" shrieks Mrs. Nuddles, as our lamprey sucks up part of her dress. "This is definitely strike two!" she yells. My mouth gets really dry.

Then, our refrigergator jumps out of my kangaroom and thwacks the lamprey with his tail. It's a good thing he hides in there whenever we have company. He licks Mrs. Nuddles to make sure she's all right.

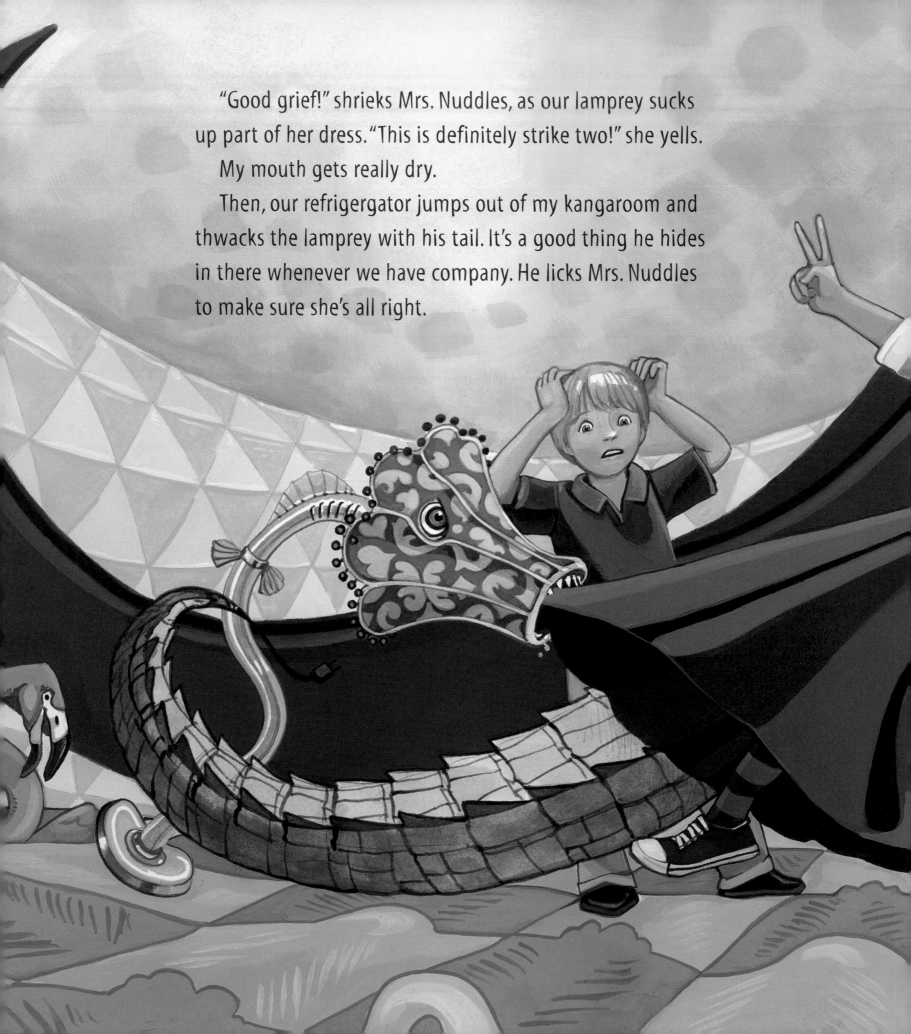

"Does this one always lick the guests?" she asks.
"Only the really special ones," I tell her. I think I
can see a small smile on Mrs. Nuddles's face.

Our refrigergator offers her a toucan of soda and a slice of magpie.

"No, thanks," she says, "but how sweet of you to ask."

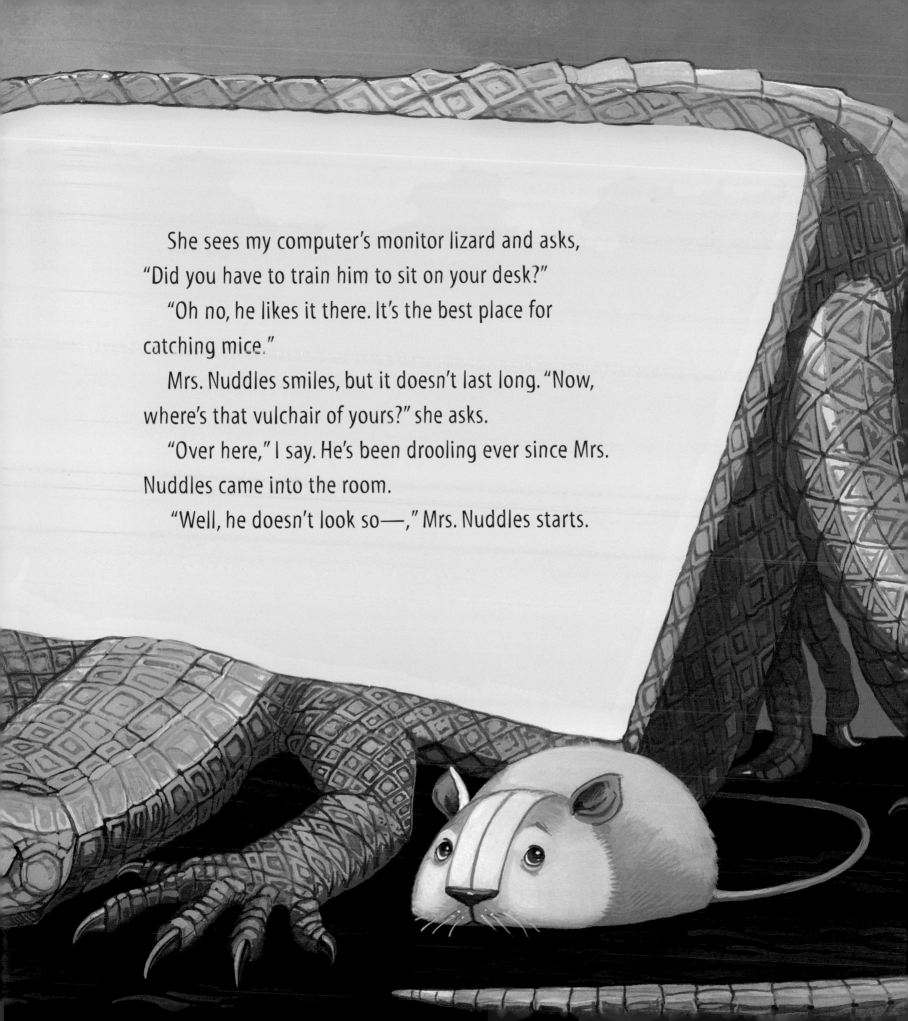

She sees my computer's monitor lizard and asks,
"Did you have to train him to sit on your desk?"

"Oh no, he likes it there. It's the best place for
catching mice."

Mrs. Nuddles smiles, but it doesn't last long. "Now,
where's that vulchair of yours?" she asks.

"Over here," I say. He's been drooling ever since Mrs.
Nuddles came into the room.

"Well, he doesn't look so—," Mrs. Nuddles starts.

And then strike three.

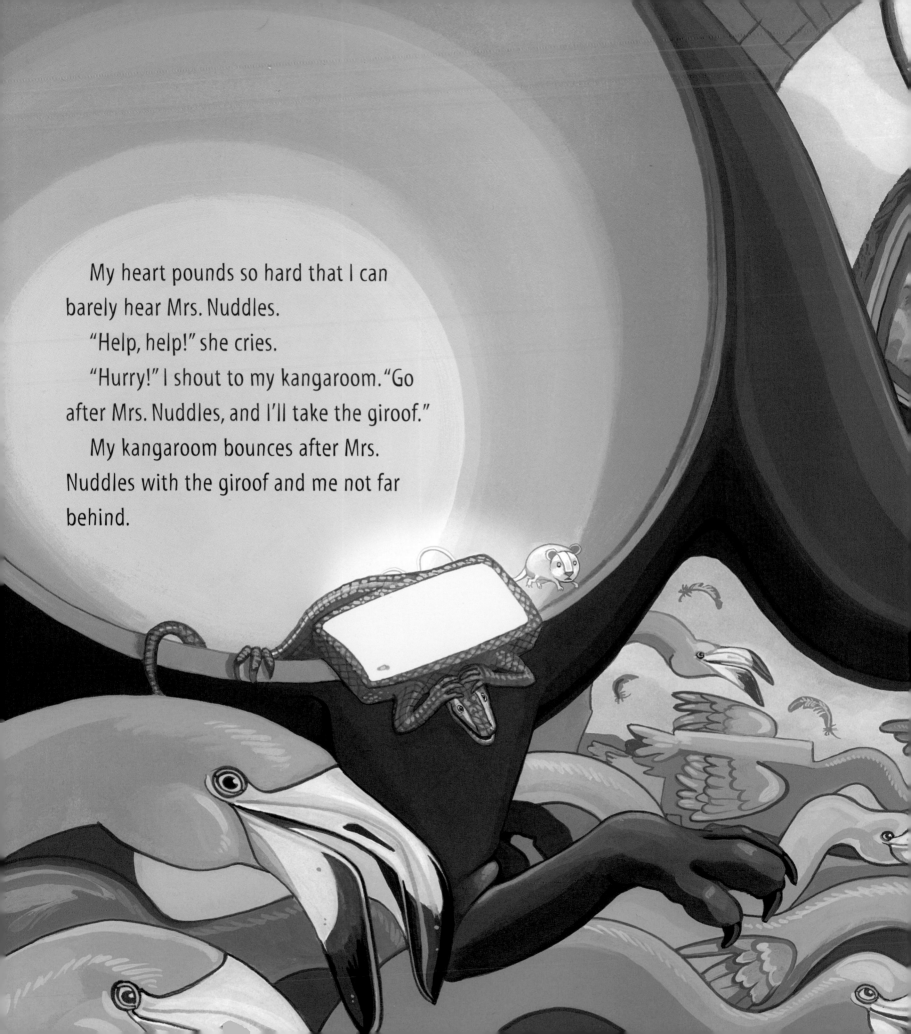

My heart pounds so hard that I can barely hear Mrs. Nuddles.

"Help, help!" she cries.

"Hurry!" I shout to my kangaroom. "Go after Mrs. Nuddles, and I'll take the giroof."

My kangaroom bounces after Mrs. Nuddles with the giroof and me not far behind.

"Quick, Mrs. Nuddles, take my hand!"

Mrs. Nuddles closes her eyes and in no time, she's with me on the giroof's neck.

"I see what you meant now about the vulchair eating your homework, but you never said anything about it eating little old ladies," Mrs. Nuddles says with a laugh, while riding back to my gorvilla.

And then she takes a really deep breath.

On her way out, Mrs. Nuddles notices Jamie watching the manatee-vee. "Your living room truly is a *living* room," she says.

"Mrs. Nuddles," I say, "about those three strikes . . ."

"I'll see you on the field trip tomorrow, Jeremy," she says with a wink. "And don't forget to do your homework."

Our refrigergator licks her good-bye.

Like I said, my teacher says I belong in a zoo, and, well, she should know. She's going to move to an anacondo on the other side of the hedgehog row.

But, best of all, I got to go on the
field trip to the mooseum.

COWCH

Remole Control

Media Storage Rackoon

BeaVo and RayStation

MAGPIE

WELCOME BAT

Jeremy's house is full of extra animals. Can you find them all?

Kangaroom

MICROWAVE

CHIMPNEY

BEARBECUE

BACK · PERCH

BIG BED WOLF

HAMPSTER

GABULL

HARECASE

BOARWAY

SATELLITE FISH

LIGHTBULBBLE FISH

Quailt

SNAILBOX